OLLIE ESCAPES the GREAT CHICAGO FIRE

BY SALIMA ALIKHAN
ILLUSTRATED BY JACQUI DAVIS

STONE ARCH BOOKS
a capstone imprint

Published by Stone Arch Books,
an imprint of Capstone
1710 Roe Crest Drive
North Mankato, Minnesota 56003
capstonepub.com

The name of the Smithsonian Institution and the sunburst logo
are registered trademarks of the Smithsonian Institution. For more
information, please visit www.si.edu.

Library of Congress Cataloging-in-Publication Data is available on
the Library of Congress website.
ISBN: 9781663911889 (hardcover)
ISBN: 9781663921376 (paperback)
ISBN: 9781663911896 (ebook PDF)

Summary: Twelve-year-old Ollie is struggling to get by as an
orphan in 1871 Chicago. He found work as a servant for the
wealthy Burnham family, including caring for five-year-old Leo
Burnham. But Ollie's own little sister, Eliza, is in an orphanage,
and he's saving every penny he can to get her out and care for
her himself. Then a massive fire breaks out in the city, and chaos
descends. Suddenly Ollie must not only escape the burning city
with little Leo, but he must also find his lost sister among the
wreckage. Will Ollie's wits and bravery be enough to save the
Burnhams' son and his own sister?

Designer: Sarah Bennett

Our very special thanks to Tim Winkle, Curator, Division of
Cultural and Community Life, National Museum of American
History, Smithsonian. Capstone would also like to thank Kealy
Gordon, Product Development Manager, and the following
at Smithsonian Enterprises: Jill Corcoran, Director, Licensed
Publishing; Brigid Ferraro, Vice President, Education and Consumer
Products; and Carol LeBlanc, President, Smithsonian Enterprises.

Capstone would also like to thank Sergeant Frederick Gordon
of the District of Columbia Fire Department.

Printed and bound in the USA. 4608

TABLE OF CONTENTS

Chapter 1

A Lucky Break

October 8, 1871—Sunday evening

"Almost finished, Ollie?" Mrs. Burnham called as she came into the parlor.

"Yes, ma'am," Ollie said, glancing up from the desk. "We're just finishing up Leo's lessons."

The Burnhams' five-year-old son, Leo, looked very relieved about that. He was slouched next to Ollie in his fine mahogany chair, kicking at the legs and sticking out his lip.

"I'm tired of lessons, Mother," Leo said.

Ollie ruffled Leo's hair. Ollie was proud of himself. He had only been working for the Burnhams for six months, and he was getting better all the time at learning how to manage all his daily duties, which included tending to Leo and giving him his lessons. By now, Ollie figured he was almost as good at his duties as a grown-up would be, even though he was only twelve. He knew how important it was to keep his job. And that meant keeping the Burnhams happy.

"We can end for today, ma'am," Ollie said, closing his book. "Leo did well."

"Wonderful," said Mrs. Burnham. "And did you finish polishing the silver?"

"Yes, ma'am." Ollie stood and helped Leo to his feet. "I'll get Leo to bed soon. I just need to clean the wagon first. Morris put the horse away already."

"Thank you. I'll come kiss you good night in a bit, Leo," said Mrs. Burnham, bustling off again.

"Will you tell me a story, Ollie?" Leo asked, gleeful now. Leo adored Ollie, and looked up to him like a big brother.

"I sure will," said Ollie. "I'll come up as soon as I've cleaned the wagon."

At least they are a nice family, Ollie thought to himself as he rounded the outside of the Burnhams' mansion to where the family's wagon stood. He could see their groom, Morris, leading the horse to the small barn. The Burnham house sat in the Washington Square Park neighborhood of Chicago, near the Mahlon Ogden mansion on Walton Street, which was just as impressive as the Burnhams'. Ollie had never thought he'd see a place this grand, let alone live in it.

He knew he was lucky that the Burnhams

had taken him in. He knew plenty of orphans that hadn't fared as well. Ollie's dad had died a few years ago in the Civil War—the war between America's Northern and Southern states—while fighting for the Union Army in the north. Then, a year ago, his mom had died of a disease that attacks the lungs called tuberculosis. Ollie's father had been a carriage driver for the Burnhams, who were charitable people. When Ollie's mother died, they kindly gave Ollie a job helping the footman and the housekeeper. Once they saw how good he was with Leo, they expanded his duties to taking care of Leo, as well.

Ollie squinted around the neighborhood. The huge elm trees around Washington Square swayed in the hot, dry wind blowing up from the southwest. It hadn't rained in months. He nervously scanned the sky. Chicago was a busy, bustling place full of wooden buildings and raised wooden

sidewalks. Many of the buildings had roofs made of tar or shingles, which caught fire easily. There had been lots of fires in the city lately—more than twenty in just the past week. It was because of the dry air, and because of all the wood.

Ollie swept out the wagon, making sure there were no traces of dust or dirt, then came back to find Leo waiting for him at the foot of the stairs. Mr. Burnham walked in and gave his young son a smile.

"Did you learn your numbers with Ollie today, Leo?" Mr. Burnham asked.

"I learned all the way to one hundred," Leo said proudly. "But we mostly did reading."

"Good boy. Off to bed with you, then," said Mr. Burnham. "Mother and I will be in to say good night in a moment."

Ollie led Leo upstairs to his room and got him dressed for bed.

"Don't forget my bedtime story," Leo said as he climbed into bed.

Ollie smiled. He set the oil lamp he'd brought up with him onto the table. Then he started telling Leo one of the stories his mother used to tell him, an old fable with witches, kings, and queens.

Leo listened with wide eyes.

Ollie never told Leo, but his heart always felt heavy when he told these stories. They made him think of his little sister, Eliza. While Ollie had found employment with the Burnhams, Eliza, who was only eight, had been put into a home for orphans, a few blocks from the courthouse. Ollie had wanted to beg the Burnhams to also take in Eliza, but he knew he was lucky to get the position he had. He could not ask for their charity.

The Burnhams had given Ollie a chance, but it wasn't common for wealthy families to adopt the siblings of their servants. He knew several siblings who had been separated after their parents died. Often, older siblings were able to work while younger ones were sent to orphanages. There just weren't many places for young orphans to go.

So it was going to be up to Ollie to save Eliza. He had made a plan to work as much as he could and get an education himself. When he had saved up enough money, he would collect Eliza from the orphanage, and he would take care of her. He was all she had.

The Burnhams let Ollie visit Eliza every Sunday for an hour, so at least he still got to see her. But he missed his sister badly. And he knew she missed him too.

Little Leo fell asleep before Ollie could finish, which often happened. Ollie tucked him in, grabbed the oil lamp, and left the room, tiptoeing across the wooden floor.

He headed to his own room, climbing the last flight of stairs to the small attic space.

Ollie sank down in his little chair. His bones felt tired, like they did at the end of every day. There was a photograph of Eliza on his bedside table. It had been taken after their parents died. Eliza wore their mother's beloved silver bracelet on her wrist in the photo, but she had no smile. She had always been so lighthearted when both their parents were alive. But ever since they had died, it was like Eliza's light had gone out.

The resolve hardened in Ollie's heart. He would get her out of the orphanage and keep her with him. And somehow, he'd also find a way to continue his education. He'd earn enough money to take care of Eliza and make sure she was never alone and scared again.

He pulled out the book he'd borrowed from Mr. Burnham's wonderful library, *Alice's*

Adventures in Wonderland. Reading was one of the few luxuries Ollie had. Mr. Burnham knew how much Ollie loved to read, so he let Ollie borrow books. So far, Ollie had read *Mark the Match Boy*, *Little Women*, *Great Expectations*, and *Uncle Tom's Cabin*.

Ollie must have fallen asleep as he read, because the next thing he knew, he was slumped in his chair, and the book had fallen to the floor. His first thought was that he'd done what servants were never supposed to do, which was to fall asleep in their uniform. Servants couldn't risk getting them wrinkled or torn.

There was a frantic knocking on the door.

"Ollie!" Josephine, one of the housemaids, burst into the room. Her face was pale and frightened. "Ollie, there's another fire! Down south. The family is packing to leave!"

Chapter 2

An Unexpected Wake-Up

"What time is it?" Ollie stumbled to his feet, bleary-eyed. Beyond his open bedroom door, he heard raised voices downstairs.

"Half past one in the morning," Josephine said.

Ollie staggered after her down the stairs, glad he'd broken the rules and fallen asleep in his day clothes—even wearing his shoes.

The house was in chaos. People were shouting, Leo was crying somewhere, and servants were yelling.

"Another fire, this one monstrous," Mr. Burnham called when he saw Ollie. "It's jumped the south branch of the river. The gasworks exploded more than an hour ago. Some people think it won't jump the main branch of the river too, but we won't take chances. The firemen are overwhelmed. Not enough of them, and not enough water! Go and help Morris pack the wagon, Ollie. Quick!"

"Ollie!" Leo, partly dressed in his day clothes again, ran over wailing and threw himself at Ollie. "Are we all going to burn to death?"

Ollie gave him a quick hug. "It's all right, Leo. We'll make sure none of us burns to death."

Ollie left poor little Leo howling in the foyer. He hurtled outside to find Morris loading bundles of clothing and food from the larder onto the wagon, which was already hitched to the horse. The horse was skittish, scuffing the ground, snorting and sniffing the air. Next to the wagon, Morris had piled trunks and more bundles to load.

To Ollie's shock, the sky had taken on a strange reddish hue in the south.

"This is a bad one," Morris said. "Some folks aren't worried, but it's jumped the river once already."

"What are they doing?" Ollie cried, pointing toward Walton Street and the Mahlon Ogden mansion. People were piling something against the side of the building.

"Wet carpet," Morris explained, heaving a trunk onto the wagon. "To prevent the flames from catching."

"But—" Ollie caught his breath, "if the fire is south—I have to get my sister!"

Eliza was still at the orphanage, right in the path of the fire!

Before Morris could say anything, Ollie raced inside and found Mr. Burnham.

"Sir," he panted. "Please. I need to go and get Eliza. She's in the path of the fire!"

For a terrifying moment, Ollie was afraid his master would say no, and that he would be forced to disobey and lose his job in order to save his sister.

But after a moment, Mr. Burnham nodded.

"Of course," he said. "You must go to her, Ollie."

Ollie sprinted out of the house and ran south down Clark Street. Eliza's orphanage was just south of the main branch of the river.

He saw several people standing on rooftops, watching the fire to the south, shouting that it would never jump the river and come to the North Side. The farther south he went, though, the more chaotic things got. The red in the south sky was creeping north and getting brighter.

And then he heard a child's scream behind him. "Ollie!"

Ollie turned. Leo was standing in the middle of the street!

Ollie's heart stopped. "Leo!" he cried, running up to him. "You shouldn't have come after me!"

Leo clung to Ollie. "Come back home," he begged.

Ollie's heart thundered even more. He glanced north, toward safety. Could he stash Leo somewhere close by while he ran to get Eliza? Quickly, he realized this was a terrible idea. Across the bridge, buildings were already catching fire. That meant many of them were already collapsing too. But he didn't have time to bring Leo all the way back to the Burnhams and then turn around again to go get Eliza. A good servant, he knew, would bring Leo back to his parents. But Ollie was not going to let

Eliza die. If he wanted to rescue her, it was now or never. With any luck, it would be quick, and then they could just hurry back north.

"Leo," he said. "I'll bring you back to your parents, but first I need to get my sister. If you want to come with me you'll have to be very brave and run very fast. All right?"

Leo nodded again and took Ollie's hand, then batted at the air as more embers rained down on them.

"Come on!" Ollie said. Together they raced toward the orphanage.

Chapter 3

To the South Side

Ollie crossed the Clark Street Bridge as quickly as he could, pulling little Leo along with him. Already some panicked people were racing north. Ollie and Leo jostled past them as they headed the opposite direction. The heat grew more intense, and Ollie felt his first twinge of doubt. The sky looked like blood in the south. Rooftops burned. His heart lurched. Had he made a mistake in bringing Leo?

The moment they were off the Clark Street Bridge, he turned left and raced east, toward the orphanage. Swirling embers and whorls of fire drifted through the air, landing on his face and clothes. He did his best to brush them aside, but still they singed his skin. The air was stifling hot, and smoke stung his lungs.

"Keep your head down and protect your face, Leo!" Ollie called, tightening his grip on the little boy's hand. He led Leo right into the thick of the crowd, dodging the ash and embers that swirled in the air as thick as snow. He tried not to get trampled by the tide of people stampeding around them and the animals frantically pulling carts.

Ollie had seen many fires in Chicago, but never anything like this. The South Side was being eaten alive, he could see that much. People were fleeing from the south, screaming and rushing toward the bridges, loaded down with belongings. Some were in carts and wagons, but many were on foot. He passed a fire engine, with several exhausted-looking firefighters trying to hose down a raging rooftop fire. It obviously wasn't working.

The orphanage was a few blocks east. Surely they had evacuated the orphans already—but where would they take them?

For the first time in his life, Ollie saw every kind of person there was in the city, all smashed together. People of all different races. There were poor orphans, like him, next to ladies dressed in fine clothes and jewelry. He saw one lady with a birdcage, and several people helping sick or older relatives. He saw some carrying mattresses on their backs. Other people dropped their belongings in order to run faster against the hot, swirling winds. Everyone wailed and shouted in panic.

"The opera house is burning!" he heard someone moan.

"And the courthouse!" someone else yelled.

The courthouse! Ollie's heart plunged again.

Little Leo was red-faced and coughing,

but he ran along as quickly as his short legs could carry him. It seemed like it took forever to battle their way to the familiar block with the rickety wooden orphanage.

"Here it is, Leo!" Ollie cried.

Then Ollie gasped. A small part of the orphanage's roof was already in flames! Ollie knew it was a matter of time before the roof collapsed and the whole building caught fire.

Then he saw two nuns shepherding some children away from the building. One of them looked up. He recognized her—Sister Margareta, who ran the orphanage.

He dashed over to them.

"Where's Eliza?" Ollie cried.

"We couldn't find her," Sister Margareta said, her face covered in ash and soot. "We got most of the children out, but there were some we couldn't find. We just came back to look for those. We called and called for her,

but she didn't come. We had to get the others out. I'm sorry, Ollie."

Ollie looked at the burning building and balled his fists. "She's in there! I know she is!"

"It's going to collapse, Ollie—you'd best run to safety!" Sister Margareta turned as if to hurry off with her train of children.

Ollie thought of something. "Please, Sister Margareta, will you watch over Leo for just a moment? This is Leo Burnham, John Burnham's son. I'm going to find Eliza. Leo, stay with Sister Margareta."

Before either of them could protest, Ollie launched into the building. Heat singed his skin, and the dark smoke burned his eyes and lungs, making it hard to see and harder to breathe. He started coughing. He heard the creak of beams.

"ELIZA!" he screamed, coughing. "It's me, Ollie!"

He waded deeper into the smoke, listening to the crackling beams above him. He shouted Eliza's name again and again.

After a few horrible seconds, he heard coughing, and then a small voice called out. "O-Ollie?"

"Eliza!" He plunged toward the voice.

He pushed past scattered furniture until he got to the back corner. It looked like a roof beam had already fallen. And the voice was coming from underneath it!

"Ollie, I'm stuck!" he heard the voice say.

He staggered toward her. The small, sooty figure of Eliza was crumpled in the corner. A fallen beam had pinned her leg to the floor. Above them, more beams creaked as the fire crawled over the roof.

"I tried to run after everyone, but this fell on me," she gasped.

Coughing even harder, almost blind now

from the smoke, Ollie bent and grabbed the beam. With all his might, he hoisted it off her leg. It was so heavy his back and legs ached from the effort, but he let out a sigh of relief when he saw Eliza wriggle out from under it.

The roof above them creaked again, and a shower of embers rained down. Ollie ignored the stinging little burns they made on his face and head. He grabbed Eliza's arms and dragged her out of the corner. When they reached the middle of the room, another beam cracked and fell—right where Eliza had been pinned.

"Can you walk?" Ollie asked between coughs. Eliza winced and cried out but held on to him and limped forward. Together, they made their way out.

Sister Margareta was still outside, holding Leo's hand. Her eyes widened as the two sooty figures came tottering out of the building.

"Eliza!" she cried and embraced her. "Where were you?"

"In the back corner. My leg was stuck." Tears streamed down Eliza's face, leaving tracks in the dark smudges on her cheeks.

"I'm so glad you're all right. You ought to hurry, children!" said Sister Margareta. "You're welcome to come with me to meet Sister Elise and the other children. We're headed east."

Ollie bit his lip. "No, I have to go north and get Leo back his parents. But thank you!"

As Sister Margareta nodded and rushed off, Ollie took Eliza's and Leo's hands. His own eyes and lungs still burning, he looked down at them and despaired. Leo was so little, and Eliza was hurt. How fast would they be able to run?

But they had no choice. He headed north with them.

"Where are we going?" cried Eliza, doing her best to limp-run.

"North," Ollie shouted. "The Rush Street Bridge!"

The Rush Street Bridge was close. But the crowd surrounded them, slowing their pace. The screams behind the threesome grew louder. Whorls of fire leapt from rooftop to rooftop. More roofs fell, and buildings crumbled. And now, horror upon horrors, strange, high pillars of fire could be seen reaching from the ground up to the sky, like mini-tornadoes.

"Fire devils!" shouted one man as he staggered past them.

Ollie could never have imagined the scene at the Rush Street Bridge—the chaos, people crammed as tightly as sardines, wailing and shrieking. Some fell from the bridge, or were pushed by the mass of people, and plunged into the cold water below.

Ollie steered as close to the middle of the bridge as he could, so neither of the children would fall off. "Hold on to me tight!" he shouted at both of them. Gripping their hands as tightly as he could, he plowed through the crowd. He felt as though he didn't breathe again until they had made it safely across, along with a slew of hundreds of other panicked people.

"It's jumped the north branch!" someone ahead of them screamed. "Fire's jumped the river!"

Ollie turned to see. It looked as if the water itself was burning—great swirling flames on the river.

He thought about how terrified Leo's parents must be, wondering where their son was.

"Come on," he shouted at the children. They started running as fast as Eliza's hurt leg would allow. It felt safer to be moving again after being stuck on the bridge. They raced up Rush Street, dodging people right and left.

"The North Side'll be swallowed!" Ollie heard a man shout. The man changed direction and raced east.

Just then, a massive sound thundered through the air—a huge, clanging shock. The sound seemed to vibrate the ground.

"What is that?" Eliza cried.

"I don't know," Ollie said, his nerves jangling.

He thought about how thirsty he was, and then he thought about water. That gave him an idea. He turned right on Ohio Street. "This way!" he said. "We're going east!"

Chapter 4

Into the Lake

"Where we going now?" asked Leo, trying to keep up on his short legs.

"To the lake!" said Ollie. Lake Michigan! Surely that would be a safe spot? He was so thirsty and hot he would have given anything for a drink of water. Why hadn't he thought of the water before? The lake would save them.

But the fire jumped the river already, said the little voice inside his head. Will the lake burn too? He knew it was probably the oil and debris floating on the river that had caught fire. It meant the fire could follow them into the water, like some kind of nightmare.

But the lake was big, and it was their only hope of getting away from the fire that raged behind them. He gave up dragging Leo and hoisted him up to ride piggyback. Carrying Leo made Ollie's lungs burn even more. Next to him, Eliza bit her lip bravely, sweat running down her face as she hobbled along. But her chin was set.

Ollie squeezed her hand. He was so relieved to have her with him. She gave him a quick look back, and he saw that her eyes were full of determination too.

"The bell tower of the courthouse collapsed!" Ollie heard someone shouting as he ran by.

The bell tower had fallen! *That's the noise we heard!* Ollie felt the shock ring through his body all over again. The city had believed the courthouse was fireproof.

Flames waved in the sky as the fire seemed to chase them, leaping from roof to roof. The North Side was burning. People shrieked as more buildings crumbled all around them.

Eliza stumbled and fell. "I can't run anymore, Ollie," she gasped. "My leg."

Ollie looked around, panicked. A wagon rumbled past, loaded with belongings.

"How much for a ride to the lake for these two children?" Ollie called to the driver.

The man looked them up and down. They were all covered in soot, but Ollie was still wearing his fine servant's clothing.

"It'll cost you," said the man, narrowing his eyes.

Eliza frowned at him. "Here," she said. She took off her mother's silver bracelet—the one keepsake she owned—and thrust it at the man.

Ollie wanted to stop her, but he knew she

was right. Getting to the lake alive mattered more than a bracelet.

The man snatched it from her. "Climb on," he said impatiently.

Eliza clambered onto the back of the wagon. She immediately looked relieved to be sitting. Ollie lifted Leo on too. Leo scooted close to Eliza, who put her arm around the little boy protectively. Ollie walked alongside the wagon as it trundled on, glancing anxiously over his shoulder. The fire was still devouring the buildings behind them. He wished the cart would go faster.

"State Street is burning!" someone shouted down the street.

"Are we all going to burn?" Leo cried.

"No," Eliza told him. "Ollie's here. He'll get us to safety."

Suddenly, there was a jolt, and the wagon pitched abruptly to one side.

Ollie had seen this happen before—wheels popping clear off of wagons.

"Come on!" Ollie said. He pulled Eliza and Leo off again. "It'll take too long to fix. We have to keep going!"

"But we gave him Mother's bracelet!" Eliza cried. "He should give it back—he didn't even take us all the way there!"

"It got us closer, at least," Ollie said, even though his heart ached. "And our lives are more important!"

As the driver stalked around the wagon, muttering angrily, Ollie pulled Eliza and Leo down the street and into the crowds. Ollie's chest was tight with worry. They would have to get to safety on their own.

This time, he hoisted Eliza onto his back.

"You'll have to run with me, Leo, because Eliza is hurt," Ollie said. "Can you do that?"

Leo nodded, and they took off as quickly

as Leo could go. The heat at their backs grew worse and worse as they hurried down Ohio Street toward an area that had once been called The Sands. Ollie had been told it had been full of gambling and criminals before the city had cleaned it up. Ollie could see the businesses up ahead that faced Lake Michigan. Beyond those, he glimpsed the narrow beach, and the boats bobbing in the water.

The lake! Just a little bit farther, and they would be safe.

But when they got to the shoreline, they saw how many people were there already. Hundreds? Thousands? Families, animals, all trapped there, between the great Lake Michigan and the burning city.

The heat and smoke pushed at their backs. "Come on," Ollie said.

They staggered across the sand, making

their way through the throngs of people and toward the water. Ollie set Eliza down. All around them, other people were plunging into the water, trying to escape the heat.

Ollie grasped Leo's and Eliza's hands and marched right into the water—then stopped.

The water was icy cold. Chills shot up his legs. His teeth started chattering.

He knew immediately that there was no way they'd survive for long in the lake.

Chapter 5

New Plans

The heat at their backs was so bad that the three of them inched farther into the lake anyway, following the other people. The air above felt like a blast furnace, but the water below was unbearably cold. There was no relief.

Leo was so short that soon the water was up to his neck and he was gasping at the cold, so Ollie picked him up. Eliza stood shivering next to them in her thin nightdress. Ollie kept an arm around her to keep her warm. He tried not to think the thing he was most afraid of—

that they wouldn't last very long out here in the frigid water.

They turned to watch the city burning— the fire raging across the buildings, the flames shooting into the red sky, the embers showering down. Around them, people in the water and on the shore were crying out. They were losing everything.

Ollie tightened his grip on Eliza. *Thank God we're here together*, he thought.

She was shivering harder than ever, though. Her lips were turning blue.

Ollie looked around, desperate for a solution. At the shore, a woman was pushing a small rowboat into the water. She had a child with her—a little boy about Leo's age. She helped her son into the boat, then climbed in herself.

"Please!" Ollie splashed over to her, holding tightly to Leo on his back and dragging Eliza with him. "Please, can you take these two? They won't survive the cold!"

He felt so desperate he was almost in tears. He couldn't stand thinking they might have come all this way only to die in the freezing water.

The woman in the boat gazed at Eliza, blue-lipped and shivering. Then she looked at Leo, who clung to Ollie and cried softly.

"Quickly," she said. "The three of you come aboard."

Ollie felt something inside him let go. Tears streamed down his face in relief as he helped the two younger ones into the boat. Once they were both inside, he felt like he could breathe again. He scrambled on board after them, trying not to tip the boat over.

When all were in, the woman began to row.

"I can help with that, if you need me to," Ollie offered, wheezing.

"You just rest for now," the woman said.

Ollie sat, his legs shaking. He couldn't quite let himself believe they'd made it to safety.

When they'd gone far enough out that the air felt a bit clearer, the woman said, "Now, we wait. My husband, Ned . . . I don't know where he is. He went to get my mother to safety, and I wanted to wait for him, but the flames came so near our house that we had to leave."

Ollie sat close to Leo and Eliza and rubbed their arms to keep them warm.

"Where are you from?" the woman asked.

Ollie took a deep breath. He thought again about how Leo's parents must be worried sick. He told the woman about rescuing Eliza and Leo. Her eyes widened as he spoke.

"You did all that yourself, child?" the woman said. "You're brave as can be!"

Ollie was surprised. The last person to call him brave had been his mother, just before she died.

The woman's little son, who looked as exhausted as Leo, leaned against his mother and fell asleep. Leo was already asleep against Ollie. The woman, Ollie, and Eliza kept watching the burning city. Soon the sun was rising, and still they waited. Near shore, people continued to plunge into the lake, seeking escape from the heat and flames.

Ollie didn't know how long they sat there. All that day and far into the next night, waiting, listening to people moaning and wailing. They grew thirsty and their stomachs growled. They took small sips of lake water to quench their thirst. Ollie worried about illness from the damp chill and from drinking the dirty water. But the fire raged on, making a return to shore impossible. Huge piles of lumber in the south began to burn, and clouds of cinders and smoke rolled over the lakeshore, making them cough and sputter.

They rowed out as far as they dared when

the smoke drifted toward them. They watched as some people drove their wagons right into the lake and then climbed on top of the wagons to avoid the cold water. Many people turned their backs to the fire and smoke, but Ollie couldn't stop looking at it.

With every new arrival, more news spread, sending jolts through Ollie's heart.

"The bridges have burned," someone shouted.

"The Water Works is burning," someone else cried.

Until, finally, after it was dark again, it started to rain.

Cheers rose from the people in the lake. Ollie lifted his face to the rain, wondering if it was real.

"Is it raining?" Eliza asked sleepily, looking around.

"Yes," Ollie said, awed. He opened his mouth

and gulped as much of the clean rain as he could. He'd never felt anything so glorious in his life.

* * *

When the fire was at last doused by the rain, people began slowly making their way back to shore. The mother who'd taken them into her boat rowed back to the beach and helped them clamber out. She asked if they needed help. Ollie thanked her for everything and told her they would be all right.

He took Eliza's and Leo's hands again and led them through the rain and back into the city. Even in the rain, the rubble they passed was still hot and smoldering—too hot to get close to.

Somehow they managed to stumble wearily to a church that hadn't burned. People poured inside, bedraggled and looking lost, trying to get out of the rain.

"Come on." Ollie could hardly stand, he was so tired. He led the children to a corner. "We'll sleep here tonight."

He kept a tight grip on both of them as they slept. When they woke up, they left the church and headed back to the lakeshore. Ollie had already heard reports of looting, and he wanted to keep the children off of the city streets as much as he could. They would walk along the lakefront until they could cut west toward the Burnhams', he decided.

They walked north, dazed and disbelieving. When they got to Chicago Avenue, they turned left and went west.

He didn't recognize the city. Eliza looked around with wide, startled eyes as they made their way carefully through the streets, rubble, and ruins. Heat radiated from the debris. On every face they passed, Ollie saw exhaustion and shock. Every once in a while he heard people cry out—in horror or in relief—because they'd discovered that their house had burned, or they'd found a loved one, or they'd found that their home had survived by some miracle.

"Everything's gone," Leo said, gaping around.

"The city is ruined," Eliza said, gripping Ollie's hand.

Street signs had burned, so Ollie had to guess at where they were. He picked his way carefully through the streets, leading the children back toward Leo's family. He was afraid of what they'd find there, but he also didn't know where else to go. He knew the Burnhams had a country house to the north of the city, but he didn't know how to get there, or if that was even where the family had gone.

His stomach twisted. *What must the Burnhams be thinking? Did they think Leo was dead?*

"I'm so hungry," Leo whispered.

"Me too," said Eliza.

Ollie's stomach rumbled too. None of them had eaten for at least two days. And he had nothing to give them.

"We'll find food soon," he said. Eliza nodded, hollow-eyed.

When they finally got to Washington Square Park, he was stunned. The first thing he saw was the Ogden mansion—the only house still standing in the area. He wondered if those soaked carpets had worked!

All around, though, other houses were in ruins. The Congregational and Unity Churches had also burned.

And, of course, the once-grand Burnham house was hardly more than a pile of smoldering rubble. Ollie could only stare.

"My house!" cried Leo.

"I'm sure your family got out and is safe," Ollie finally managed to say, hugging the boy and hoping what he said was true.

Ollie tried not to think what would become of Eliza and him now. Even if the Burnhams offered him a place in their country home, there was no way he could go, and be so far from Eliza.

And where would she go? The orphanage was also likely gone. Nervous sweat coated his brow. He decided he and Eliza would leave Chicago and go west into the prairie, rather than send Eliza to another orphanage.

"Ollie?" came a voice. "Ollie? And—Leo? Oh my goodness, is that my Leo? Leo!"

Ollie craned his neck at the sound of the familiar voice. Mrs. Burnham was picking her way through what was left of their home. She rushed up to them and swept Leo up off the ground.

"My boy!" she cried. "John—he's all right! Thank heavens!"

Mr. Burnham came behind her, stumbling over fallen beams. They'd come back in their wagon. Ollie could see Morris.

"Ollie saved me!" Leo said to his parents. "And he saved Eliza."

Mr. Burnham turned in amazement to Ollie. "Ollie, what happened? We looked everywhere! We . . . we held out hope that you were together." He cried in relief as he hugged his wife and his son.

Ollie was so tired and hungry he wanted to collapse. "Mr. Burnham, I'll tell you the whole tale. But right now, I'm sorry to trouble you, but I have to ask if you have any food with you? My sister and Leo haven't eaten since the fire started. Nor have I."

"Of course, of course. We brought food, hoping we'd find you." Mrs. Burnham carried Leo over to the wagon. She rooted around, pulled out a basket with bread inside, and handed each child a piece.

It was the best food Ollie had ever tasted. He tore into his piece. Eliza, too, ate as though she'd never eaten before.

"We stayed at the Lionels' place north of Lincoln Park," Mr. Burnham said. "We were going to go to the country house, but we didn't want to leave the city without Leo. We've been everywhere, inquiring at every possible place for him. And to find him here! Ollie, please, tell us what happened!"

Feeling a tiny bit better with the bread in his stomach, Ollie told them. Leo and Eliza helped, adding some details. With every word, the Burnhams' eyes grew bigger.

When he was finished, Mrs. Burnham's eyes were filled with tears. She hugged Leo all over again. Mr. Burnham laid a hand on Ollie's shoulder.

"You've been a hero. You saved our boy,"

he said. "Ollie . . . we were going to offer you a post in our country home, of course, since you're so good with Leo. But, I think I have a better idea. Why don't you and Eliza come with us? I'll explain on the way."

* * *

Four days later, Ollie found himself on what was probably the most important ride of his life. He and Mr. Burnham were in the wagon, driving across town to visit one of Mr. Burnham's friends.

Ollie's newly starched collar was stiff against his neck, and he tugged at it to help himself breathe. All around them, the city was in ruins. The rubble had cooled, making it safer to inspect now. Newly homeless people were sleeping in churches or in tents that had sprung up to house them. Martial law had been declared, and soldiers had been called to the city to make sure there was no more looting or plundering. Troops patrolled the streets.

It was bleak and grim, but already people were rebuilding. Relief societies were being created to help. Some of the banks were already back in business, operating out of temporary shelters. The *Chicago Tribune* hadn't wasted any time—they had already printed an edition about rebuilding the city.

The Burnhams' wagon pulled into a small row of houses on the West Side that had been spared from the fire.

A kindly looking older gentleman greeted them at the door.

"Howard Wilcox." The man shook Ollie's hand with a smile. "You must be Ollie. Mr. Burnham tells me you're the hero who rescued his son and your own sister. Why don't you come in, and we'll talk business?"

"Um, yes, sir," said Ollie. He felt strange

about being called a hero, but they followed Mr. Wilcox into his parlor, which was full of books.

"I was most impressed to hear about your bravery, Ollie," said Mr. Wilcox.

"Um . . . thank you," said Ollie, flushing.

"I also hear you're excellent with children and good at teaching them their lessons," said Mr. Wilcox.

"Yes." Ollie nodded. He was proud of that—he was good with children.

"We're very lucky that our school didn't burn," said Mr. Wilcox. "But my aide had to flee the city with his family. I want to ask, would you like to be my new aide, in exchange for room, board, and pay? You would live in comfortable rooms above the school."

Mr. Burnham had told Ollie that Mr. Wilcox was thinking of making him an offer like this, but Ollie still felt speechless.

"Y-yes, thank you," Ollie said. He cleared his throat, wondering if he could get the words out. "I'm very honored. But, I have a request."

Mr. Wilcox raised his eyebrows. "Yes?"

"My sister Eliza," Ollie said, trying to keep his voice steady. "We're orphans. I don't want to send her to another orphanage. Could she stay with me, and become one of your pupils? She's very bright and won't cause any trouble."

"I think that could be arranged," said Mr. Wilcox, smiling.

"Ollie had another request as well," said Mr. Burnham. "Go on, Ollie."

Ollie took a breath. "And if—if you don't mind, sir—I'd like to continue my own education as well. I'll work very hard for you, but I would like to be able to follow lessons along with the older children, and to study in the evenings when I'm finished with my duties."

Mr. Wilcox's smile grew slowly. "You're hungry to be educated! Excellent. I think we can manage all of that. I would be happy to tutor you myself on more advanced subjects."

Ollie let out a huge, shaking breath. "Thank you, sir. I'll work very hard."

"I have no doubt you will," said Mr. Wilcox.

"And Leo will attend your school as well," Mr. Burnham added. "He will be very happy to see Ollie every day."

Ollie and Mr. Burnham thanked Mr. Wilcox and said goodbye.

"Life is sometimes not fair," Mr. Burnham said as the wagon trundled back through the Chicago streets, "but occasionally, heroic deeds are rewarded. Mr. Wilcox recognized that and believes courage is important. You deserve this opportunity, Ollie."

"Thank you, sir," said Ollie, still marveling at what had just happened.

Mr. Burnham gazed around at the ruined buildings.

"The city will rebuild," he said. "Better than before. Better fireproofing, better safety measures. Chicago will become greater than ever."

"Yes, I think so, sir," said Ollie.

The wagon pulled up to the Lionels' house, where they were all staying for a few weeks. Soon the Burnhams would move to their country home while their new house was being built in the city.

As the horse came to a stop, Ollie saw Eliza in front of the house, waiting to hear the news. Ollie hopped down from the wagon. He couldn't wait to see his sister smile again.

THE GREAT CHICAGO FIRE

The Great Chicago Fire of 1871 was one of the most devastating fires in American history. That fall had been unusually dry and hot, and there were wooden buildings and sidewalks all over the city that burned easily. At that time, Chicagoans were used to fires. But they still weren't prepared for a terrible blaze that would leave miles of the city in ruins and more than 300 people dead.

It hadn't rained in months, and there had already been at least 20 fires in the city that week. Firefighters were exhausted from battling all the blazes. Then, on the night of October 8, 1871, a fire began in a barn on the South Side of Chicago.

This time, conditions were perfect for a furious blaze. The fire spread from the barn and tore through the city. By the time rain began to fall on October 10, the fire had left a trail of destruction in its wake, burning a section of the city about one mile wide and four miles long. It destroyed 17,000 buildings, killed more than 300 people, and left about 100,000 people homeless.

Many people displayed great courage in helping family, friends, and strangers to safety. Survivors described it as terrifying, otherworldly, and awe-inspiring in its size. The sky glowed red, and the fire rained smoldering embers as thick as snow flurries. Many of Chicago's most beloved buildings, several of them believed to be fireproof, crumbled and fell. The fire even jumped the river and burned on the oily water.

As people struggled to flee the flames, the fire brought the rich and the poor, the immigrants, politicians, and merchants, all together for a brief period. Servants and lawyers, grandmothers and babies, railroad workers, businessmen, and children all fled in terror, trying to save what they could.

The late nineteenth century was a time in American history when people were very racist as well as "classist," meaning that it was believed that your value and importance were entirely based on your wealth and status in society. They were also very divided in their social and ethnic groups. Tensions ran high. Many of the city's working poor—laborers, immigrants, and the roughly 4,000 Black people living in the city at the time—were considered "beneath" the wealthier white classes. This was despite the fact that these groups had built most of the city, and contributed culture, art, and ideas. Many native-born white Chicagoans held deep prejudices against immigrants and people of color.

During the fire, though, all people were reminded how short life can be. Many of these social classes mixed for the first time as people fled the fire.

After the fire, people got to work rebuilding their lives. Within a week, 6,000 temporary buildings were built. The *Chicago Tribune* newspaper continued to publish the paper from a makeshift office amidst the rubble. On October 11, just a day after the fire was out, they published an edition with a headline that pronounced: "Cheer Up . . . looking upon the ashes of thirty years' accumulations, the people of this once beautiful city have resolved that CHICAGO SHALL RISE AGAIN." Within a decade, Chicago had indeed rebuilt a bold new city with safe, fireproof buildings.

GLOSSARY

chaos (KAY-oss)—complete disorder and confusion

civil war (SIV-il WOR)—war between opposing groups within one country

debris (duh-BREE)—the scattered pieces of something that has been broken or destroyed

evacuate (eh-VA-kyuh-wayt)—to leave an area during a time of danger

larder (LAR-dur)—a place where food is kept

luxury (LUHG-zhuh-ree)—something that is not needed but adds great ease and comfort

martial law (MAR-shul LAW)—control of people by the government's military, instead of by the civilian forces, often during an emergency

monstrous (MON-struss)—large and frightening

orphanage (OR-fun-nij)—a place that provides a home for children whose parents have died or cannot care for them

parlor (PAHR-lur)—a formal living room

shingle (SHING-uhl)—a thin piece of building material, often with one end thicker than the other, for laying in overlapping rows as covering for a roof

tuberculosis (tu-BUR-kyoo-LOW-sis)—a disease caused by bacteria that causes fever, weight loss, and coughing; left untreated, tuberculosis can lead to death

MAKE A FIRE ESCAPE PLAN

Fires can spread so quickly that people often have less than two minutes to escape after the smoke alarm sounds. There are many things you can do to make a home fire escape plan!

1. **Look** at every exit and entrance. What are the quickest and easiest ways to get outside? What is the best escape route from each room? Draw a floor plan of your house to help you decide.

2. **Find** at least two ways out of each room. Where are the doors? The windows? Are the windows safe to climb out of, or are they too high up? Second-story windows will need fire escape ladders.

3. **Keep** escape routes clear, and test to make sure the windows open easily.

4. **Plan** a route for anyone with a disability to get outside safely.

5. **Make** sure there are smoke alarms installed in every sleeping room, outside each sleeping area, and on every floor of the house.

6. **Choose** a meeting spot a safe distance from your house where everyone should meet in the event of a fire.

7. **Practice** your home fire escape plan a few times a year with your family. It's good to be prepared!

ABOUT THE AUTHOR

photo by Sam Bond Photography

Salima Alikhan has been a freelance writer and illustrator for fourteen years. She lives in Austin, Texas, where she writes and illustrates children's books. Salima also teaches creative writing at St. Edward's University and English at Austin Community College. Her books and art can be found at www.salimaalikhan.net.

ABOUT THE ILLUSTRATOR

photo by Jacqui Davis

Jacqui Davis was born in Johannesburg, South Africa, and moved to the United Kingdom as a child. Jacqui has been producing art for children's books and board games since 2012, after studying animation at Staffordshire University. She enjoys painting everything from adorable animals to villainous wizards. She currently lives and works in Lytham-St-Annes, which is great for walks through the woods or ambles along the estuary.